The Curse
of the
Squirrel

By Laurence Yep
Illustrated by Dirk Zimmer

A STEPPING STONE BOOK

Random House New York

To Simon,
who doesn't eat anything
that can have fun.

Text copyright © 1987 by Laurence Yep. Illustrations copyright © 1987 by Random House, Inc. All rights reserved under International and Pan-American Copyright Conventions. Published in the United States by Random House, Inc., New York, and simultaneously in Canada by Random House of Canada Limited, Toronto.

Library of Congress Cataloging-in-Publication Data:
Yep, Laurence. The curse of the squirrel. (A Stepping stone book) SUMMARY: From the time a giant squirrel curses Farmer Johnson's best hunting dog, things are never the same around the farm, and hunting little animals ceases to be a sport. [1. Hunting—Fiction. 2. Animals—Fiction] I. Zimmer, Dirk, ill. II. Title. III. Series: Stepping stone book (Random House (Firm)) PZ7.Y44Cu 1987 [Fic] 87-4612 ISBN: 0-394-88200-8 (pbk.); 0-394-98200-2 (lib. bdg.)

Manufactured in the United States of America   2 3 4 5 6 7 8 9 0

Contents

1

A Hound Among Hens

Farmer Johnson stepped out of his house. In one hand he held a lantern. In his other hand, he had his gun. He gave a low whistle. "The sun has set and it's a possum moon," he said. "Let's go hunting, boys and girls."

Howie the Hound woke under the porch and crawled out. "I'm up!" he yelped.

Farmer Johnson couldn't understand animal talk. He just looked around. There should be more dogs than Howie. "Where is everyone?" he wondered.

Howie threw back his head and gave a howl. "It's time to run," he announced. "It's time to hunt." Howie was very proud of his voice. It was deep. It carried across the whole farm, but the other dogs did not answer. "That's odd," Howie said to himself. "Why don't they say something?"

Farmer Johnson snapped his fingers. "Find them, Howie."

Howie sniffed the night air. He recognized the smells of the other dogs. "This way," he barked to Farmer Johnson.

Howie led him to the chicken coop. The other dogs were standing around it, and they were laughing.

"Why are you wasting time?" Howie asked them. "The master wants to hunt."

One of the other dogs was called Boon. He turned and said, "Your brother is in the chicken coop, and he won't come out."

Howie ran and pushed his way past the other dogs. Then he looked through the little doorway. "Willy," he said, "you're not a chicken. You're a dog. Come out of there."

Willy burrowed deeper into the nest of straw. Only his eyes and black nose showed. "It's too dangerous outside," he said.

The other dogs began to make fun of Willy.

"Willy is a chicken!" Queeny yelped. "Come on and cluck for us."

Boon sneered. "Lay an egg, Willy."

Howie was very brave. Willy was very tim-id. Howie always had to protect his brother. "No one makes fun of my brother," Howie said. He nipped Boon and the other dogs.

"Ow, ow, ow!" The other dogs ran off a few yards.

In the meantime, Farmer Johnson got down on his knees and peeked through the door. He saw Willy in the nest. "Willy, you don't have feathers. You don't lay eggs. Get out of that coop."

Willy just stayed. "No, no. Beware of Shag."

Howie wriggled underneath Farmer John-son so he could look through the door too. "I've hunted in the forest for years," he said. "I've never heard of him."

Willy lifted his head. "He's a giant squir-rel. He came to the forest last night," he said. "I won't leave the farm. It's too dangerous. Shag is out there somewhere."

"Don't play games, you silly dog." Farmer Johnson stepped into the coop.

Howie scolded his brother. "How many times do I have to tell you? Don't speak to squirrels. Squirrels are our enemies. You can't trust them."

"These squirrels were my friends." Willy hid back in the straw. "And they were all very upset. Shag eats all the nuts when he comes to a forest. Then he leaves."

Farmer Johnson reached into the straw and grabbed the back of Willy's neck. "Willy, you're more trouble than you're worth." He tried to drag Willy out.

The nest of straw was inside a wooden crate. Willy clung to the sides of the crate. "No, no, no," he barked. "It's too dangerous. Stay home."

"I'll protect you, Willy," Howie coaxed. "I always do."

Farmer Johnson tugged at Willy, but Willy bit one side of the crate. Farmer Johnson lifted Willy up. Willy lifted the crate up. The farmer gave Willy a little shake. "Let go of the crate, Willy."

Willy just bit deeper into the crate.

"Let go." Farmer Johnson's face turned a bright red. He shook Willy even harder.

Willy's teeth sank deeper into the wood.

"I'll make you let go, you silly dog." Farmer Johnson gave Willy a good shaking. Straw went flying all around the coop. A tiny piece of straw tickled Farmer Johnson's nose, and he sneezed.

Farmer Johnson had a very big nose, so it was a very big sneeze. It made him take a step backward. He tripped over Howie.

"Ouch!" yelped Howie.

Down went Farmer Johnson. Up went Willy.

Farmer Johnson sat down on another nest. The chicken flew away just in time. "Oof," the farmer said as Willy fell on his lap. Willy's crate landed on the farmer's head.

The frightened chickens flew everywhere inside the coop. Many little feathers floated in the air with the straw.

Farmer Johnson squirmed. His voice was muffled because there was a crate on his head. "I feel something wet. I think I'm sitting on an egg."

He lifted the crate from his head and saw

all the chickens flying around. "Now my chickens are upset. They may not lay any more eggs for days."

Howie poked his head in through the doorway. "It's still not too late, Willy. Come with us."

Willy shook his head. "I saw a paw print from last night. It was the footprint of a squirrel and it was as big as me."

Howie touched noses with Willy. "Some smart squirrel dug it to fool you. All the forest animals are laughing right now."

Willy's eyes grew very big. "I heard noises, too," said Willy. "Big thumps. It was a giant squirrel walking."

Howie entered the coop. "It was the squirrels," he said. "They drummed on a hollow log. Let's teach those squirrels."

"Shag is out there," Willy insisted. "I can feel it."

A chicken settled on the farmer's head. Farmer Johnson looked up at the chicken. The chicken looked down at Farmer Johnson. That was all the farmer could stand. "I have egg on my pants, and now a chicken is nesting on my head." He glared down at Willy. "And it's all your fault."

"I'm sorry," Willy whined.

Farmer Johnson shoved Willy off his lap and got up. "Willy, you're a crazy, useless hound. I'm going hunting. When I come back, I don't want you on my farm."

"I have to go with him," Howie told his brother sadly.

Willy crept back into the crate. "Be careful," he answered.

2

Shag Takes a Nibble

Howie led the other dogs into the woods. The night air was fresh with exciting smells.

The other dogs nosed about. "Here's the scent," Boon said eagerly.

"No, it's over here," said Queeny.

All the dogs ran around and argued.

Howie was the best tracker. He did not waste time arguing. Instead, he searched silently. Finally he smelled possum. The grass held the scent. It was strong. It was recent. Howie would catch the possum. He would run faster than the wind. He would leap higher than the stars. The possum could not escape him.

"I have the scent," he barked to the other dogs in his deep voice. "Follow me."

Howie was also the quietest and quickest dog. He soon left the others behind. Only the moon could stay with him. It was almost full now, and it floated above the treetops like a huge, fat balloon.

Howie raced into the heart of the forest where the trees grew close together. Their tops hid the moon now. "I've outraced even the moo-oo-oon," Howie bayed.

The forest around him was strangely silent. No owls hooted. No other animal moved. Still Howie ran on through the darkness.

Suddenly his sharp ears heard a thumping sound. It sounded like a giant animal hitting his foot on the ground.

"The squirrels might have fooled Willy," Howie muttered. "They won't fool me. They're just beating a hollow log." He got angry—so angry that he forgot about the possum. "I'll teach you to play games with my brother." He ran toward the sound. He thought he would catch the squirrels soon. Instead the noise grew louder.

Thump. Thump. Thump.

"There must be a lot of squirrels beating the log," Howie thought, running along faster and faster. The bushes whipped past him.

Feathery ferns tickled his belly and legs.

Thump! Thump! Thump!

He leaped into a clearing and then raised his head angrily to howl. "You can't foo-oo-ool me!"

The other dogs answered in the distance. "No, you-ou-ou can't. No, you can't."

Suddenly the bushes shook in front of him. A thin sapling crashed to the ground. *Ka-thump! Ka-thump! Ka-thump!*

A squirrel stepped into the clearing. It was the largest squirrel Howie had ever seen. Howie had to lean his head back to see the squirrel's face. It stared down at him with glowing red eyes.

"H-h-hi," Howie stammered.

Humans could not understand animal talk, but all the animals understood one another.

"How do you do," the squirrel said in a deep voice.

Howie began to back away. "I don't think we've been properly introduced. My name is Howie."

"My name," the squirrel said, "is Shag."

"And a good name it is." Howie backed off a little farther. "Welcome to the forest."

"You mean that I'm welcome because you want to catch me. Then it's into a human stewpot." The squirrel narrowed his eyes angrily.

"No, no, I prefer salads myself." Howie was almost near the bushes now.

"And you look like a big furry walnut to me." With one huge bound, the squirrel was right next to Howie. Its paws knocked Howie flat on his stomach. Howie glimpsed two huge white teeth. They gleamed in the moonlight. He gave a frightened yelp as he felt the teeth sink into his shoulder.

"Hold on! Hold on! We're almost there!" the other dogs yelled in the distance.

"Here I come, Howie!" Farmer Johnson shouted.

Shag frowned. "This forest is too crowded." He let go of Howie. "You're cursed now, Howie. By day you will be a dog. But on nights when the moon is full, you will become a squirrel—a big one, just like me." Shag walked off into the bushes.

Howie got up.

The other dogs came into the clearing. "What happened?" they asked.

"I met the giant squirrel," Howie said. "He bit me."

The other dogs did not say anything for a long while. Then Queeny cleared her throat. "It looks like a raccoon clawed you."

"It was a giant squirrel," Howie said. "Look at the size of the tracks."

Queeny shook her head. "You said that was a trick. Don't make up stories about giant squirrels. Just admit that you're scared of raccoons."

"We have to get away from here right away," Howie warned.

The other dogs looked at one another. Queeny whispered quietly to the others, "Howie's lost his nerve."

"You're all fools," Howie snapped.

Farmer Johnson huffed and puffed his way into the clearing. He was very fat and did not like to run. Howie limped over to his master. "What happened?" the farmer asked.

"It's dangerous," Howie barked.

Farmer Johnson did not understand Howie. But he did see Howie's wound. "Poor boy," he said. "Let's go home." He picked up Howie and left. The other dogs followed.

Runaway Cabbages

Willy was not home when they got back.

Farmer Johnson carried Howie into the kitchen and washed Howie's wound. Then he put a bandage on it. He spread an old blanket on the floor and lay Howie down on it. Finally he gave Howie a bowl of water.

"Rest up, boy. You're my best dog." He patted Howie on the head and went upstairs to bed.

When the sun rose the next day, Howie went to look for Willy. Howie asked everyone from the chickens to the cows, but no one knew where Willy had gone. He wanted to search for his brother, but his shoulder ached. "I'll be stronger tomorrow," he decided. "I'll look for him then."

On the way to the house, he passed by a field of cabbages. His nose had never twitched before, but it twitched now. He could not stop it. His nose twitched like a squirrel's. "No," he said. "I am a dog. My nose is just itchy. I am not a squirrel. Shag is a liar."

The cabbages were round. Walnuts are round too. In fact, the cabbages reminded him of big green walnuts. All his life he had ignored cabbages and walnuts. He went into the field and patted a cabbage. "Why didn't I notice it before? Nuts and cabbages have the perfect shape."

He tried to go, but the cabbage seemed to whisper, "Don't desert me, Howie. Birds and insects will eat me. The sun will wither me. I'll lose my perfect shape. I won't look like a nut then."

Howie turned around. "I'll save you, cabbage. I'll put you away. No one will touch you. You'll stay perfect like a nut."

With his nose and paws, he pushed the cabbage from the field. Then he rolled it along.

An oak tree grew near the barn. The tree was so big and old that there was a space under its roots. Howie rolled the cabbage into it.

"There!" Howie declared. "You're safe now."

The cabbage sat like a sad green walnut. "Howie," it begged, "save my brothers and sisters."

The space under the tree seemed so big, and the cabbage seemed so little. The cabbage was right. It needed company. "I'll save them, too," Howie said.

When Farmer Johnson visited his cabbage field later that day, most of the cabbages were gone.

"Help! Cabbage thieves!" Farmer Johnson yelled.

The dogs immediately ran to him.

"It's the pigs!" Boon shouted. "They're greedy."

"No, it's the cows!" Queeny yelped. "I never did trust anything with horns."

Every dog blamed some other creature as the thief.

Farmer Johnson pointed at the tracks. "These belong to the thief. They look like a dog's, but they can't be. No dog steals cabbages."

The dogs followed the tracks. Farmer Johnson followed the dogs. They went straight to Howie. He was sitting in front of the old oak tree. He felt all the cabbages in back of him.

"Howie, there's a cabbage thief," they said.

"How terrible!" Howie said.

"Help us find him," the dogs urged.

Howie had never told a lie in his life. But he thought of all his cabbages under the tree. He had promised to save them.

"I think a rabbit went into the woods," Howie lied.

"You didn't chase him?" they asked.

"My shoulder hurts," Howie explained.

Boon ran around in a circle. He came back to Howie. "The tracks end at this tree," he said.

"He did it in one hop," Howie said.

All the dogs stared at him doubtfully.

"It was a big hop," Howie added.

"What're you doing here, Howie?" Queeny asked.

"Just relaxing." Howie tried to study the clouds in the sky.

"What's in the tree, Howie?" Boon asked. He tried to nose past Howie.

Howie growled and showed his teeth. "Nothing," he said.

"You're acting weirder than your brother," Farmer Johnson said. "Get away from that tree, Howie."

Howie moved over an inch.

"More," Farmer Johnson ordered.

Howie moved another inch.

Farmer Johnson patted his leg and said, "Come over by me, Howie."

Howie had never ever disobeyed Farmer Johnson. He could not do it now. He got up.

Everybody heard a funny sound.

Suddenly a hundred round, green cabbages rolled from the tree. They swept Howie off his feet. They carried him right over to Farmer Johnson.

The cabbages and Howie hit the farmer's legs at the same time.

"Oof," Farmer Johnson grunted, and fell backward. The cabbages picked up Howie again and took him along. Both dog and cabbages rolled over the poor farmer.

Twenty yards away the cabbages stopped. Howie picked his way through the cabbages back to his master.

Farmer Johnson still lay there. He had an odd look on his face.

Howie hung his head in shame. "Maybe there is some kind of curse on me," he said. "I've never talked to cabbages before and I've never stolen or hoarded them."

Howie licked his master's forehead. Then he waited for Farmer Johnson to get mad and call him names, but Farmer Johnson just stayed on his back.

"I have seen many strange things in my life," Farmer Johnson finally said. "I have caught a two-headed snake. I have grown a pumpkin in the shape of John Quincy Adams. But I have never, never had a dog that hoards things like a squirrel."

He got up slowly. "I will go to bed. When I wake up, the world will be normal again."

He took one step. Unfortunately, his foot touched a cabbage. This time he fell forward. He stared at the dirt while he spoke. "I won't rush. I'll even crawl, but I'll make it to my bed."

He rose again and wiped the dirt from his face. "Good afternoon," he said to the dogs, and slowly went back toward his house.

4
Outcast

"You've shamed us," the other dogs said, "but we forgive you. Your wound must hurt you."

Howie crept under the front porch. He wanted to hide from everyone. The farmer's words had frightened him. He was acting like a squirrel. Could Shag's curse really be working? He would be a dog by day, but he would be a squirrel when the moon was full. Maybe the closer it got toward sunset, the more he would act like a squirrel and less like a dog.

His nose started to twitch again. "Stop that!" he said to his nose, and clapped two paws over it.

Then, even though his paws covered his nose, he smelled something delicious. He sniffed the air. It was coming from the kitchen.

Howie sneaked around to the kitchen

steps. The kitchen was empty and the door was open. He crept into the kitchen. On the table was Farmer Johnson's lunch.

Howie's shoulder still hurt, but he jumped up onto a kitchen chair. Farmer Johnson had made some peanut butter sandwiches. They sat on a plate. The peanut butter jar was by the plate.

It was strange. Howie had never liked peanut butter before. Now the smell made him drool. He licked the drop of peanut butter on the butter knife. It was wonderful!

"Farmer Johnson will never miss one sandwich." He gobbled up a sandwich.

The peanut butter was crunchy and chewy. It tasted of hot, sunny fields. It tasted of lazy afternoons. It was the taste of growing.

Howie looked at the second sandwich. The peanut butter looked even thicker on that one. "Farmer Johnson needs to go on a diet," he said. He ate it in two bites.

The third sandwich was the fattest of them all. "It looks so lonely," Howie sighed. He ate the third one too. Then he licked the stray peanut butter from the plate.

The smell of peanut butter still filled the kitchen. The lid was loose on the jar. Howie could see all the peanut butter inside it.

"I'll just see if it's fresh," Howie said. He licked the outside. The jar moved an inch toward the edge of the table.

"Did I miss a spot?" He licked the jar again. It moved another inch.

"The jar really has an interesting shape." His tongue felt the jar. Closer and closer he shoved the jar toward the edge. Suddenly it teetered on the side of the table and fell with a crash.

"They used to make jars stronger in the old days," Howie said. "Well, Farmer Johnson won't want the peanut butter now." He climbed down off the chair and began to lick up the peanut butter on the floor.

The noise had awakened Farmer Johnson. He came to the kitchen door. He saw the empty plate. Then he saw the broken jar.

Howie smiled in apology. Peanut butter covered his muzzle.

"Howie, you are the weirdest dog," said Farmer Johnson. He opened the kitchen door

and pointed outside. "Get out. I will clean up this mess, but you are no longer welcome in my house."

Howie slunk out of the kitchen. Shag had spoken the truth. Howie really was cursed. He now liked the taste of nuts. Even worse, he could not control himself. He was acting like a squirrel!

The other dogs were waiting at the foot of the kitchen steps.

Howie hung his head. "I shamed all dogs today," he said.

"You are no longer our leader," the other dogs said.

"I understand," Howie said. "I have to wait for my shoulder to heal. Then I'll go. No one will ever see me again." He crept back under the front porch.

5
Full Moon

Howie stayed under the house all that day. The other dogs avoided him. When the sun set, Farmer Johnson got up and had dinner. Then his big boots thumped on the boards overhead. When he whistled, the other dogs yelped, "Let's hunt! Let's run!"

Howie did not crawl out from under the porch, and Farmer Johnson did not look for him. Neither did the other dogs. They left without him.

Howie could hear them argue in the distance. Boon barked, "Here's the scent."

Queeny whined, "No, it's here."

Without Howie to lead them, the dogs could not agree. They argued and argued. They were still arguing as their voices faded away in the forest.

"Willy," Howie sniffed, "where are you? I

miss you." He fell asleep.

The moon came out. It shone down on the farm. Its silver light crept across the farmyard and under the porch. The light surrounded Howie. It soaked through his skin. He began to itch all over. "Ah-choo," he sneezed. His muzzle and ears shrank. His tail and hind legs lengthened. His two front teeth grew until they hung over his lower lip.

"I don't feel well," Howie said. He looked
at his front paws. They looked like squirrel
paws.

"What's happening?" He reared up. His
head hit the porch. Crack! The boards broke.

"Ow." Howie got back down on all fours
and crept out from under the porch. When he
was finally in the farmyard, he sat back up.
He tried to wag his tail, but it got caught on
a rosebush.

He turned his head. His tail was big and
fluffy. "That is a . . . a squirrel's tail." Howie
freed it from the rosebush. He felt his ears and
his muzzle. They didn't feel like a dog's. They
felt like a squirrel's.

"Oh, no! I really am a squirrel." Howie
tilted back his head. He wanted the whole
world to know how sad he was. He tried to
give a deep howl. It only came out as a loud
"Ch-ir-r-r-k." Even his wonderful deep voice
was gone.

"This is the final insult." A big tear
splashed down his cheek. He absently used the
tip of his fluffy tail to wipe his eye.

Right then Howie heard Farmer Johnson
coming back. "Where are all the animals?"
Farmer Johnson cried. "Are they all hiding?"
He sounded tired and disgusted.

Howie sat down. "Thank goodness. Now
Farmer Johnson can take me to the veterinar-
ian."

Then Howie heard Queeny coming. "Wait!
I smell squirrel," said Queeny. "The scent is
very strong. Maybe there are lots of them."

"We'll show them! They can't hide from us!" the other dogs shouted.

Queeny led the dogs around the barn. She skidded to a halt when she saw Howie. The rest of the dogs were still running. They bumped into her and tumbled into a pile.

"Yipe! Yipe! Yipe!" they yelped.

Farmer Johnson finally came around the corner. "Holy Hannah! It's a giant squirrel."

Howie realized that the farmer meant him! "No, no." Howie raised his forepaws. "It's me, Howie. See my bandage? It's still on my shoulder."

"You can't fool us," Boon said. "You must be Shag. Willy told us about you. You ate Willy. You ate Howie."

Farmer Johnson rubbed his eyes. "This is a bad dream. I'm not here. I'm home in bed." He pinched himself. "Ow. Darn it. I'm awake." He looked at the other dogs. They were lying on their bellies and whimpering in fright. "I really am seeing a giant squirrel."

Howie walked over on his hind legs. He wanted to sound dignified. He wanted to sound calm. He wanted to sound like a dog, but his squirrel's voice only sounded high and funny in that giant body of his. "Something is wrong. Help me."

Farmer Johnson was so scared he shook all over. He couldn't even aim his gun steadily. "Keep away, monster."

"I'm no monster," Howie said. "I'm the best hunting hound. Look at me." He took a step closer.

Farmer Johnson backed away in terror. He lifted his gun and fired. He missed Howie, but he did hit the rosebush. Flowers and leaves showered down.

"Yipe," Howie tried to say. Of course, he could only chatter. He turned around. His big tail twitched in Farmer Johnson's face. Farmer Johnson gave a big sneeze.

"I really am cursed," Howie said miserably, and ran toward the forest. He needed some safe place where he could think.

Farmer Johnson watched the giant squirrel run away. Then he went inside his house, picked up the telephone, and called the sheriff. "Come out quick," Farmer Johnson said.

"The biggest squirrel in the world just tried to bite me. It was the size of a cow."

The sheriff chuckled. "I've hunted squirrels for thirty years. No squirrel is that big."

"It was just on my farm," Farmer Johnson protested.

"You're drunk," the sheriff laughed.

"I'll show you," Farmer Johnson said. "I'm not drunk. There really is a giant squirrel." He hung up.

Farmer Johnson went outside. He gave a big whistle. "Come on, boys and girls. We have to hunt that squirrel."

The other dogs stayed where they were. They were very frightened. They did not want to go.

Farmer Johnson gave a grunt. "I'm going to find that squirrel. I'll do it by myself if I have to."

The dogs looked at one another. They could not let their master go by himself. They were still scared, but one by one they got up and joined Farmer Johnson.

6

The Hounding of Howie

Thistles and bramble thorns cut at Howie's legs. His big, bushy tail snagged in the tree branches. "How does Shag run through the forest?" Howie wondered.

He stopped by a pond to rest.

The moon was high and full overhead. It shone on the water. The pond was as shiny as a mirror. Howie's reflection floated up at him.

He looked at his squirrel's ears and his squirrel's nose. "No one knows me now. My own master and friends hate me."

His tears fell into the pond. Ripples spread across the surface. For a moment his reflection was gone.

"Nothing could be worse than this," he sighed.

Then he heard the distant baying of the dogs.

"What are they hunting now?" Howie wondered.

"I smell squirrel. A big, big squirrel," howled Queeny.

Howie sat upright. "They are hunting me!" he said.

He started to run again. He was not used to his big new body. Roots tripped him. Bushes caught his tail. He moved very slowly.

He also left an easy trail. The other dogs followed it swiftly. Soon they were right behind him. Their teeth nipped at his heels and tail.

"Look! He is scared!" shouted Boon. "He isn't so tough."

"I am Howie," Howie said. "I cannot fight you."

"Liar!" Queeny said. "Take your punishment like a real squirrel."

"I think that I'll just escape," Howie said. He ran faster. He trampled down bushes. He jumped over logs. The other dogs stayed with him.

He splashed along creeks. He climbed up hills. Still the other dogs howled after him.

Finally he climbed a tree. His claws bit into the bark as he went higher and higher. At last he was out of reach of the other dogs.

"We have him! We have him!" they barked excitedly.

Howie tried to crawl out onto a branch, but it was so thin that it broke underneath him. Then he tried to climb all the way up the tree trunk. The trunk got skinnier and

began to bend under Howie's weight. "Maybe I can reach the next tree," he said. "Then I can climb through the treetops."

As the tree curved over, Howie tried to grab the branch of the next tree. It was just out of reach.

A bright light suddenly shone on Howie. It was Farmer Johnson's lantern. "Treed like a possum," he said to Howie. "I got you now."

"I'm Howie!" Howie shouted.

Farmer Johnson didn't understand. He only pulled back the hammer of his gun. Howie heard the loud click. Howie had heard that sound many times before. But he had never been the target.

He closed his eyes. "Oh, Willy, Willy, where are you? You were so right. I was so wrong."

Suddenly the bushes began to rattle and a dog let out a howl. It sounded like Willy. It *was* Willy! "Another giant squirrel is coming," Willy barked.

Howie heard the other dogs take up the cry. "It's another one. It's another one."

Willy disguised his voice. He made it

sound very high, like some younger, frightened dog. "Oh, no. It's dozens and dozens of giant squirrels," he said. "Run! Run! Run!"

Beneath him, he saw Queeny race around in a panic. She always had a good imagination. "No, it's a hundred!" she said.

Boon was so scared that he even tried to climb Howie's tree. "No, it's every giant squirrel in the world!" he said.

Howie decided to frighten them even more. "You'll be sorry," he said to the other dogs. "My brothers are going to hang you by your ears from the nearest tree."

"Run! Run! Run!" the rest of the dogs said. They raced past Farmer Johnson.

Then Howie heard Farmer Johnson. "Wait for me!" he shouted. He ran after his dogs.

"Willy, are you down there?" Howie called.

The bushes stopped rattling. Then Willy stepped out into the moonlight.

"Howie? Is that really you?" Willy stared up at him. "You look just like Shag."

"I know," said Howie unhappily. "He cursed me." Howie began to climb back down the tree trunk. "Where have you been, Willy?"

"I wanted to find out how to chase away Shag," Willy explained.

"And you found out?"

"Yes, but what happened to you?" Willy asked.

Howie climbed down to the ground. "Shag bit me. Now I change into a squirrel when the moon is full."

"Maybe Auntie Jin-Jin can help you," Willy suggested. "She lives in the swamp."

Howie brushed his big tail nervously. "The swamp! No one goes there."

"I went there," Willy said. "You'll have to go there too."

Howie stared in surprise. "But you're usually so scared."

Willy scraped his paw in the dirt. Then he shrugged. "I was more scared for you."

Howie cleared his throat. "Willy, I was wrong. You are not a coward." He reached down and patted Willy on the shoulder. "Thank you."

"Forget it," Willy said. He rubbed himself against his brother. "Let's go to the swamp."

7

Auntie Jin-Jin

Howie and Willy moved slowly through the swamp. Green moss hung like ragged shirts from the old, crooked trees. Twisted branches reached down toward them like claws. The smell of the muddy water filled their noses. They had to jump from one patch of ground to another to keep from getting wet.

Howie hesitated. "This is a creepy place. You came here?"

"I went in the daytime. It's not as scary then," Willy explained.

When Howie looked behind them, he saw ripples on the water. As they went on, the ripples followed. Some underwater creature was after them.

"Something's hunting us," he whispered to Willy.

"It must be one of Auntie's pets," Willy

explained. "She keeps water snakes and alli-
gators."

Howie shivered. "Whatever it is, I don't
want to meet it."

The swamp trees grew right in the water.
Their roots looked like black snakes dancing.
Howie and Willy had to make their way over
the roots. More ripples showed on the water as
more creatures followed them. Once Willy
slipped and almost fell in. Howie caught him
just in time. They heard teeth snap shut on
the air. There was a disappointed sigh, but it
was so dark that they never actually saw the
creature itself.

Auntie Jin-Jin was a possum so old that
her fur was almost white. It bristled like little
nails.

She was hanging upside down from a
branch by her long, skinny tail. Beneath her
was a big, overturned turtle shell that she
used as a pot. Her paws looked almost like
human hands as she stirred a blue brew with
a stick. There was no fire. Even so, the brew
bubbled and gave off steam.

"Back so soon, Mister Willy?" Auntie Jin-Jin asked in a scratchy voice.

Willy's nose twitched at the smell of the brew. "My brother needs help," he said.

Auntie Jin-Jin stared at Howie. "So Mister Howie met Shag."

"How did you know?" gasped Howie.

"I know a lot of things," Auntie Jin-Jin said. "I know all about Shag. I know all about you, too. You are the greatest hunter."

"Once," Howie said sadly.

"You hunted squirrels and raccoons . . . and possums," Auntie Jin-Jin said.

Howie scratched the back of his neck. "Once," he mumbled.

"Would you again?" Auntie Jin-Jin asked.

"Of course not," Willy said quickly.

Auntie Jin-Jin smiled strangely. "Then stand in front of me, Mister Howie."

Howie faced Auntie Jin-Jin. Her little black eyes glittered. She muttered something. Then she raised her stick and struck Howie on the head.

"Ow," he said. He rubbed the sore spot. "You hit me hard."

"It is a strong curse." Auntie Jin-Jin pointed to a little gourd. "Now fill that with the brew. Take it home and paint yourself blue. Then go into your farmer's house and hang upside down."

"Into the house?" Howie asked.

Auntie Jin-Jin began to stir her brew again. "You can stay a were-squirrel the rest of your life if you like. Each month, on the nights when the moon is full, you will become a giant squirrel." She began to cackle at the thought.

"No, no, we'll do it," Willy said.

Howie filled the gourd. "Will your pets follow us?" Howie asked.

"You have been hunted now, Mister Howie. How do you like it?" Auntie asked.

"I don't like it at all," Howie said.

"Neither do we," Auntie Jin-Jin said. Her high, thin cackle followed them as they left her swamp.

8

An Evening Visitor

When they got back to the farm, Farmer Johnson was still gone. Howie and Willy crept into his house.

"Help me find some garlic," said Willy.

"Garlic?"

Willy nodded. "Auntie Jin-Jin says that Shag is afraid of it."

Howie searched the lower cabinets in the kitchen. Then he looked through the higher cabinets. He found a string of garlic hanging from a nail. "This looks pretty old," he said.

Willy looked at the string. "Is there any more?"

Howie held up a small jar with holes in the lid. "This contains garlic flakes."

Willy sighed. "It will have to do."

They went into the living room. A big, ugly lamp hung from the ceiling. "That might hold me," Howie said hopefully.

He poured brew all over himself. It stained his fur blue. It stained the floor, too. Howie pushed a chair underneath the lamp and tied his tail around the lamp. Surprised, Howie said, "It doesn't hurt to wind my tail in a knot."

"It must be some magic in the brew," said Willy.

Howie stepped off the chair and hung upside down. Drops of brew spattered the floor.

Suddenly they heard the dogs come back to the farmyard. Willy stood up on his hind legs. He peeked out the window. "Oh, no, it's Farmer Johnson."

"They can't see me like this." Howie started to reach for the chair when his nose began to itch. His whole body felt hot. Little ants seemed to crawl up and down under his skin. "Willy, I'm changing."

Farmer Johnson's boots sounded heavy on the porch. The front door started to open.

"We'll have to keep him out then," said his brother. He threw himself at the front door and slammed it shut.

"Only a little longer," said Howie. His nose began to stretch. His hind legs started to shrink. His tail got smaller and smaller. Though it was still tied around the lamp, it did not hurt yet. Auntie's magic was very powerful.

"Who's there?" Farmer Johnson demanded in an angry voice. He shoved at his front door.

"I can't hold him," Willy moaned. He was not strong enough or heavy enough. The front door flew open. Willy fell on the floor.

"It's finished!" Howie shouted happily. His ears and paws were now a dog's. A blue dog's.

Farmer Johnson stood in the doorway. His gun was in his hands. "Who's in my house? What are you doing here, Willy?" Then he saw Howie. A blue Howie. An upside-down Howie. Howie now looked like a fuzzy blue apple with long hound's ears.

Farmer Johnson lowered his gun. He simply stared.

Howie smiled apologetically. "Hello," he barked.

Farmer Johnson took a deep breath. Then he said, "You have hoarded cabbages. You have eaten my peanut butter. But you are now beyond weird, Howie."

He untied Howie from the lamp and set him on the floor. "I won't wonder about the lamp. I won't try to figure out the blue paint.

I won't even think about the garlic on my floor."

Then the other dogs began to bark outside. "The squirrel! The giant squirrel!"

Howie ran to the doorway. Shag reared his head back stiffly, and his big, bushy tail whipped back and forth. "Come on, doggies," he chattered angrily. "Come on and fight me. Come on and fight someone bigger than you."

Howie heard Queeny snarl, "Big words, Shag, but we know you're a coward. We just chased you through the forest."

"No! That was me!" Howie started to say, but the other dogs were too busy watching Shag bounce up and down angrily on his hind legs.

"I never run," said Shag.

Howie saw Boon crouch, ready to spring. "We treed you, Shag. You made up silly stories about being Howie. You were scared."

The other dogs growled their agreement.

Shag clawed the air and slowly stomped toward the house. Thump. Thump. Thump. "No doggy scares me. You're just furry windbags."

Boon sprang at the squirrel—but this was not just any were-squirrel. This was Shag. Shag slapped him away with the back of his paw. Boon went sailing head over tail through the air. When he hit the dirt, he went on rolling.

Queeny tried to bite Shag's leg, but Shag picked her up and tossed her into a bush. Before the other dogs could yelp or run, Shag charged right into the middle of them and knocked them around like old walnuts.

Howie gulped. Farmer Johnson's dogs were the best and bravest dogs in the county. Now they lay whining and yelping just where Shag had thrown them.

Shag just kept on going. He climbed right up the steps. His claws scratched the wood. His eyes were big and red. His tail flicked angrily from side to side. His front teeth quivered up and down. He was eager to bite something. He looked straight at Willy, at Howie, and at Farmer Johnson. "Now it's time for your lesson," he said.

9

Garlic

Farmer Johnson dashed for his gun. Howie and Willy dashed for the garlic.

"Stand back," Farmer Johnson said. He picked up his gun.

Shag leaped into the room and snatched the gun from Farmer Johnson's hands.

"Thanks for the toothpick. I'll use it later." Shag threw the gun into the corner.

Farmer Johnson did not understand Shag. He only heard the squirrel make angry chattering sounds. Even so, Farmer Johnson was scared. He picked up the telephone and dialed. "Help!" he said over and over.

Shag ripped the wire from the wall. "No one can save you now. I'm going to cover you with little bites. Then I'm going to dump you into a stewpot."

He grabbed Farmer Johnson's shoulders.

His claws sank through the farmer's thick coat and heavy flannel shirt. Shag opened his mouth. His teeth looked awfully sharp.

Suddenly Howie grabbed the jar of garlic flakes. He held it in his teeth as he raced over. Rearing up on his hind legs, he began to shake his head frantically. Garlic flakes flew all over Shag. They also went all over Farmer Johnson.

Farmer Johnson did not understand. He thought the garlic flakes were for him. "Now that crazy dog is seasoning me," he groaned.

Shag just sneezed. "Stop that!" he managed to say.

Howie started to jump up and down as he shook the jar. "Take that and that and that," he mumbled. He had trouble talking because the jar was in his mouth.

"Stop!" Shag yelled, and sneezed again.

Willy ran up on the other side with the string of garlic between his teeth. He began to rub it against Shag. "And take this and this and this!" mumbled Willy. Howie was proud of his brother. Willy the coward had turned into Willy the hero.

"Oh, no. Garlic!" Shag said. "Ah-choo, ah-choo. Ugh! Garlic always gives me hives." He dropped Farmer Johnson with a thud.

The poor farmer sat there and stared at his two dogs. Howie and Willy were hopping up and down on either side of the squirrel.

Farmer Johnson scratched his head. "I don't know which is crazier—a giant squirrel or two dogs with garlic."

"Stop it! Stop it!" Shag began to scratch his sides. At the same time he sneezed again and again. He scratched and sneezed for a while longer before he ran toward the front door. "I know when I'm not wanted."

The other dogs had crowded into the doorway, but Shag bowled them over like cabbages. Sneezing and itching, he ran into the forest so fast that the ground shook.

10
Strolls at Twilight

Things were never quite the same at the farm again. Cabbages, carrots, and even turnips disappeared. Farmer Johnson would find the empty holes in the ground. Then he would stare at Howie. Howie would pretend to look the other way.

Of course, Howie was the thief. He no longer liked meat. He wanted vegetables. He and Willy visited Auntie Jin-Jin one last time. Howie told her about his problem. "Can you help me?" he asked.

Auntie Jin-Jin simply stirred her blue brew. "Auntie is no fool. I cured you in my own way. The best hunter is now the best vegetarian."

"But that isn't fair," Howie protested.

Auntie Jin-Jin's eyes became cold and bright. "Is it fair to hunt rabbits and squirrels, Mister Howie? Is it fair to scare little possums? Be glad I made you just a vegetarian and not a vegetable."

It seemed that Howie was stuck.

And from that time on he was never very good at hunting. His heart was just not in it. Luckily, Farmer Johnson did not like hunting anymore either.

The other dogs changed too. They could catch nothing without Howie. They became cautious even with the smallest rabbits, and began to eat vegetables with Howie and Willy. They also ate nuts in the forest. The squirrels could hardly believe it.

Eventually Farmer Johnson just left his gun at home. He went for long walks with his dogs instead.

He always found a clove of garlic in one of his pockets. Sometimes it was hidden in his pants. Sometimes it was in his coat.

He would take it out and stare at it.

Howie would cough and shake his head.

Farmer Johnson would put it back in his pocket. Then he would walk on. Howie would be on one side, Willy on the other. The rest of the hounds followed behind.

And giant squirrels never bothered any of them again.

About the Author

LAURENCE YEP has written many widely praised books for children, including *Dragonwings*, which was a 1976 Newbery Honor Book. He has this to say about *The Curse of the Squirrel:* "I've always been a fan of classic horror movies—though I would be scared for days after seeing one. In *The Curse of the Squirrel* I finally achieved an old ambition to write a horror story of my own. But instead of being frightened, I got to laugh a lot."

Laurence Yep lives in San Francisco, where he was born.

About the Illustrator

DIRK ZIMMER was born in West Germany and began drawing comic strips and picture books when he was four years old. He attended the Academy of Fine Arts in Hamburg, traveled all over Europe, and moved to the United States in 1977. Best known for his illustration of funny, spooky books, Dirk Zimmer says he enjoyed working on *The Curse of the Squirrel* "because one of my early ancestors was a squirrel."

He lives in New York State.